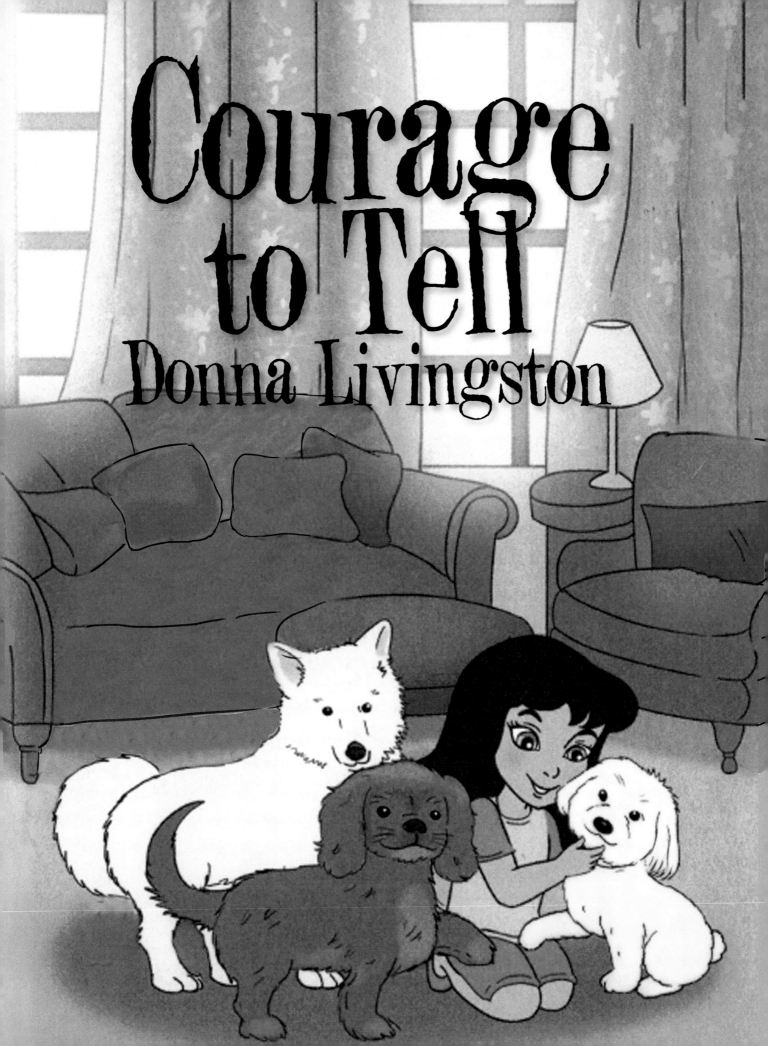

Courage to Tell
Donna Livingston

To order additional copies of this book, contact:
Xlibris
1-888-795-4274
www.Xlibris.com
Orders@Xlibris.com

I dedicate this book to my husband David, and my three children David, Desiree and Danny, my 8 grandchildren, and for the protection of all the children who are being molested and sexual abused. May this book help them tell someone so they don't have to suffer for years of abuse. I also want to thank my husband David, my daughter Desiree, my sister, Pat, and my cousin, Tara, who encouraged me to write this book. I also give praise to my Guardian Angels and God who woke me up in the middle of the night and gave me the words to write this book.

Going to Grandmom's

"Mommy, is today the day when I go to Grandmom's House?" I am going to stay overnight with my Grandmom and my uncle. They live on a farm. I love playing with the animals. I can't wait to see Grandmom's dogs, Charlie, Willie and Lance. They love it when I come to visit. They love to jump on me and kiss me. My uncle George picks me up at my house. My mom gets me ready to go stay with Grandmom for the weekend. I always have fun at Grandmom's House.

Going to the Yacht Club and Fishing

Today, my other uncle who lives at my grandmom's is picking up my brother Mickey and me. We love going to his yacht club. He has a big boat and takes us fishing. My brother and I always have to wear a life Jacket on the boat for safety. We love fishing and we caught several fish today. We even got to swim off the boat. We always have fun when we go to the yacht club. Our uncle asked us if we would like to have lunch in the yacht club dining room. We always ask if we can have a hamburger and a birch beer. It comes in a big mug, and it is delicious. Mickey and I love hamburgers and birch beer. When the day is over, it's time to go home to Mommy and Daddy.

Going to the Atlantic City Beach

Today my uncle George is taking Mickey and me to the beach in Atlantic City. We are going to go swimming at the beach. We like to build sand castles and dip our feet in the ocean. We have to be very careful of the big waves and we can't go too far out. When we are done swimming we go up on the boardwalk and my uncle buys us a pork roll sandwich. Uncle George is so nice to us. He buys us peanuts on the boardwalk and lets us go on all the rides at the pier. My brother and I love riding the roller coaster. When the day is over, it is time for us to go home to Mommy and Daddy.

Going Shopping with my Uncle

"Mommy, is today Saturday?", I asked.

"Yes it is, and your uncle is picking you up in one hour." Mom replies with a smile.

Yay! I can go to Grandmom's for the weekend. I can't wait to see the baby lamb on the farm and the dogs. The lamb says, "Baa, Baa."

"Okay Debbie, let's pack your suitcase and get you ready. Your uncle will be here soon." says Mommy.

"I think I hear a knock at the door." I say with excitement.

"Well, go and see if it is uncle George." she says

"Hi Debbie, are you ready?", he smiles.

"Oh yes, uncle George." I smile back.

"Well let's get in the car and put your seat belt on. Today we have some shopping to do at the grocery store for Grandmom, and I have to go to Macy's for a shirt."

We went shopping and Uncle George bought me Cinderella slippers. He always buys me presents and gives me money.

Happy Birthday I am 6 Years Old

Today is my birthday and I am 6. Mommy and Daddy gave me a watch and on the face of the watch is Cinderella! Mommy, this is my favorite present! Thank you! Thank you! Thank you!

I am going to Grandmom's again this weekend. Uncle George is picking me up tonight. My family has an Italian pizza restaurant and it is next door to our house. Mommy and uncle George work there on the weekends, so I get to go to Grandmom's house. Uncle George is picking me up late tonight so when we got to Grandmom's house everyone was sleeping. Uncle George carried me into his room tonight. He touched my private parts. I don't know why he did that. I got up the next morning and I saw my Grandmom, but I didn't tell her.

Why didn't I tell her?

My Grandmom would be really mad at my uncle if she knew he touched my private parts.

Grandmom made French toast with Italian bread for breakfast and it was yummy.

Boys and girls, did anyone ever do that to you? If they did, PLEASE, PLEASE tell someone right away boys and girls. OK? TELL, TELL, TELL someone.

My New Friends

I met a friend today and her name is Karen. She lives two doors up the street from Grandmom's house. Karen invited me to her birthday party next week. I am going to wear my beautiful party dress and my red sparkle shoes to her party.

Today is Karen's party and Grandmom gave me a card with money in it to give to Karen. Everyone was all dressed up. We played games and won prizes and had birthday cake and soda.

I met another girl at the party and her name was MaryAnn. I really like her and hope we can become friends too. Karen and I played every weekend when I went to Grandmom's house and became best friends. One day uncle George took Karen and me shopping. Karen and I were in the front seat of the car. Karen was in the middle and Uncle George tickled her in her private parts. I think she told her mom. She wasn't allowed to come to Grandmom's house any more. I always had to go to her house to play. Karen's mom protected her by not letting her come down to my grandmom's house. Karen was never allowed to sleep at Grandmom's house. Karen's mom kept her safe.

Boys and girls, did anyone ever do that to you? If they did, PLEASE, PLEASE tell someone right away. OK? TELL, TELL, TELL someone.

I am 10

I am now 10 years old. My uncle is still touching my private area. I've never told anyone because I didn't think they would believe me. I am at Grandmom's for the weekend again. My Grandmom walked down the street to see her friend. My uncle came into my room. He touched my private parts and I yelled NO. I told him I was going to tell my grandmom and my mom if he ever touched me again. I am now old enough to know that It is wrong for anyone to touch your private parts and hurt you. SAY NO AND YELL. Boys and girls, did anyone ever do that to you? If they did, PLEASE, PLEASE tell someone right away. OK? TELL, TELL, TELL someone.

I am 13

I am now 13 years old and live with my grandmom. I am going to high school right down the street from Grandmom's house. I never told any of my friends what my uncle did to me, I was embarrassed and ashamed.

My uncle doesn't touch me anymore but when my Grandmom goes to her friend's house, he takes off his clothes and exposes himself to me. I still don't tell anyone, not even my sister. I did find out as I got older that he molested five members in my family and he is called a pedophile. I didn't know when I was younger that it was wrong for him to touch me in my private area. I realized it when I got older, but I still never told anyone not even my grandmom. I know now that when it happens we have to tell someone. I also was being bullied in grade school and in high school. I told my sister, Pat and my friend, Chris in high school and they confronted the bullies to stop bullying me.

Boys and girls, did anyone ever do that to you? If they did, PLEASE, PLEASE tell someone right away. OK? TELL, TELL, TELL someone.

Mommies and Daddies SAFE, UNSAFE

Please read this book carefully to your children so they can come to you if a person has targeted your child. It can be a father, mother, grandmother, grandfather, uncle, aunt, neighbor, cousin, friend, brother, sister. It could be anyone. A pedophile buys a child's love. They buy presents, give money, and spin a web around their prey. Don't let this happen to your child. To keep them safe teach them the rules of SAFE and UNSAFE. Sleepovers can be UNSAFE, you don't know who might be there that you don't know. Your child can be touched by someone they know or another person at the sleep party.

UNSAFE also is when your child is walking down the street, and a person in a car comes up to your child and offers them some candy or tells them about a lost dog, and they go over and he pulls them into the car.

SAFE: Keep your children safe by making sure where they are and who they are with at all times. A cell phone is a good tool for your children so you can get in touch with them at all times, and know where they are.

BOYS AND GIRLS LISTEN CAREFULLY

TELL,TELL,TELL. If someone asks you, can I touch your private parts, say "NO, private parts are private to me" and TELL someone. If someone asks you to touch their private parts, say NO. It could be anyone. It could be your mom or dad, aunt or uncle, grandmom or grandfather, sister or brother, cousin or friend, neighbor, teacher or coach. Please go tell someone to keep you safe. I didn't know what to do but now YOU DO. TELL!!!!!!!! If you tell someone and they don't help you or believe you.

call 911

DON'T TOUCH PRIVATE AREA

I AM NOW 30 YEARS OLD

I am now 30 years old, and I finally told my sister and cousin. I talked to them about what happened to me and they were sad. I talked to my uncle who molested me, and he told me he doesn't know what I am talking about.

He lied; he wouldn't tell the truth.

I had 3 children at the time and sat them all down and told them what happened to me and please TELL ME if anyone ever touches you in your private areas I don't care who it is TELL MOMMY OR DADDY. I love you very much and I don't want anyone to hurt you.